The Atrocities

ALSO BY JEREMY C. SHIPP

Vacation
Cursed
The Sun Never Rises in the Big City

COLLECTIONS
In the Fishbowl We Bleed
Monstrosities
Attic Clowns
Fungus of the Heart
Sheep and Wolves

NONFICTION
Always Remember to Tip Your Ninja

THE
ATROCITIES

JEREMY C. SHIPP

A TOM DOHERTY ASSOCIATES BOOK
NEW YORK

THE ATROCITIES

Copyright © 2018 by Jeremy C. Shipp

Cover image by Sam Araya
Cover design by Christine Foltzer

Edited by Lee Harris

A Tor.com Book
Published by Tom Doherty Associates
175 Fifth Avenue
New York, NY 10010

www.tor.com

Tor® is a registered trademark of
Macmillan Publishing Group, LLC.

ISBN 978-1-250-16438-4 (ebook)
ISBN 978-1-250-16439-1 (trade paperback)

First Edition: April 2018

*To all my teachers over the years
who went above and beyond*

The Atrocities

Turn left at the screaming woman with a collapsing face. Turn right at the kneeling man with bleeding sores the size of teacups. If you come across a big-breasted bear with a child's head in her jaws, you're going the wrong way.

These instructions are written in gold letters, in elegant uncials. I can see the silhouettes of my fingers through the thin parchment paper.

Turn right at the woman sliced into twelve pieces. Please don't touch the statues. Please don't litter.

I weave my way through the hedge maze, dragging my faux-leather luggage trolley through the fresh-cut grass. After a while, I remove my Oxford pumps so I can feel the greenery between my toes. A mellow breeze cools my face. The air smells like lavender.

I pass a little girl with stone flames bursting from her eyes and mouth. She screams a silent scream, like all the others.

Finally, I reach the bottom of the parchment paper. The instructions say: *Walk forward.* They say: *Please don't pick the flowers.*

The path opens wide, and the hedges glare at me on either side, clipped into massive faces with wide open eyes and wide open mouths.

A little voice tells me to turn back, but a little voice always tells me to turn back.

I walk forward. I don't pick the flowers.

Before me, Stockton House scratches at the gray sky with two pyramid spires. Dozens of headless figures populate the yellowing, weatherworn facade. These sculpted figures reach to the heavens, their fingers curled. The wind picks up, dragging the heavy blanket of cloud across the firmament.

While double knotting the laces of my pumps, I spot a brown billfold crushing a patch of pale flowers. Inside the wallet there's a photograph of a small girl and a hundred-dollar bill. The girl looks a little like my son, with the big brown eyes and impish smile. A crown of lavender flowers sits askew on her dark curls. The girl reaches out for me, or for whoever took this photograph.

I approach two towering doors of black wood. An elongated woman balances on the trumeau. She's faceless, hairless. Her long, skeletal fingers press together in prayer.

A small section of the enormous door swings open, and an elderly woman bursts from the house. She's wearing a simple blue dress and a muslin apron embroidered with black feathers. Her tight gray hair pulls at the sagging skin of her face.

"Hello, miss," she says, taking hold of my luggage trolley. "Glad to see you found your way through the hedge. We had to send out a search party for the last one who came. Didn't know her left from her right, that one. I'll ask you, how can a teacher not know her left from her right? Mr. and Mrs. Evers will be glad to know you didn't have any trouble in the hedge."

The old woman turns around and disappears into Stockton House. I follow her through a brightly lit foyer with a red-and-white tessellated floor. Here and there, the tiles form geometric faces with wide open eyes and wide open mouths. For no good reason, I avoid stepping on these heads.

"You'll like it here," the old woman says. "Mr. Evers had eighty-four-inch, high-definition televisions installed in all the living quarters. I'll ask you, miss, have you ever seen your favorite program on an eighty-four-inch television? Mr. Evers is no skinflint when it comes to creature comforts. Safe to say you will like it here, miss."

The woman speeds forward as if she's walking on a moving sidewalk at the airport. I have to jog for a few seconds so that I don't lose her.

"My name's Antonia, but no one calls me that anymore, miss. My mother would call me Antonia if she were still alive, but she died from extrahepatic bile duct cancer twelve years ago. The name I go by is Robin. You might find this difficult to believe, but I can't remember who gave me the name or why. Robin's a pleasant enough name, so the history's of little consequence."

Robin leads me to a sitting room full of red velvet armchairs with carved mahogany frames. Most of the chairs face an eighty-four-inch, high-definition television mounted on the wall. A woman, probably Mrs. Evers, kneels in front of a marble fireplace. She's dressed in a chiffon evening gown with a ruched bodice. And she's using a bare hand to scoop dirt or ash into a brown paper bag.

"We had a little accident," Mr. Evers says, dressed in a gray checked suit with a wide lapel. He's standing next to the fireplace, grinning at the mound of ash on the floor.

"Let me do that for you, Mrs. Evers," Robin says, racing forward.

"No, no," Mrs. Evers says, waving away the old woman. "I'll do it. I don't think Grandfather would appreciate being swept into a dustpan." She continues scooping handful after handful of what must be her grandfather's ashes into the paper bag. On the mantle above Mrs. Evers's head rest a number of large white urns. Human faces protrude from the front of the urns, their eyes closed and their mouths downturned.

Mr. Evers approaches and takes my hand. He squeezes

tight. "What did you think of the Atrocities?"

"Atrocities?" I say.

"The statues in the hedge maze. Job, Lot's wife, the Levite's concubine, etcetera, etcetera."

The back of my hand itches, but I don't move. "They're . . . interesting."

"They're dreadful, aren't they?" Mrs. Evers says, standing. She holds her ash-coated hand as far away from the rest of her body as possible. "I would have ground the things into gravel years ago, except Hubert has a soft spot for tourists." Robin hands Mrs. Evers a towel the same color red as the armchairs surrounding us. "Once a year, we open the hedge to the public. People come from all over the world. It's really quite strange, the number of them willing to fly thousands of miles to see hideous statues."

Mr. Evers clears his throat. "What Mrs. Evers fails to grasp is that the Atrocities are more than mere grotesqueries. They exude historical and spiritual significance. Back when Stockton House was a church, the entire congregation would travel the maze together, hand in hand in hand. The parishioners would stop and reflect on every Atrocity. And what would they see? Not a hideous statue. They would look beyond the violence and suffering to the metaphysical core of the image. They would see a manifestation of God's power." Mr. Evers clears his throat again. "Forgive me for droning on. You must be exhausted after your flight."

"Oh," I say. I pull the wallet from my pocket. "I found this outside. There isn't any ID, so I'm not sure—"

"Didn't I tell you she would return it?" Mrs. Evers says, pulling the wallet from my hand. "Her references are more than impressive."

I let out a huff of air before I can stop myself. They purposefully left the wallet outside for me to find?

"You'll have to forgive the unorthodoxy of our little test." Mr. Evers sits on one of the velvet armchairs, and motions for me to do the same. "You see, Ms. Valdez, we require a governess with very specific qualifications. And this goes beyond a mastery of math and science and linguistics. As we mentioned in our letter, our daughter is having a difficult time coping with her present . . . circumstances. She is, for lack of a better word, degenerating."

"Isabella's frightened, and she's acting out," Mrs. Evers says. She bites at a fingernail on the hand she used to scoop up the ashes.

"Yes." Mr. Evers polishes his glasses with a handkerchief the same red as the armchairs. "Isabella is a troubled child, and we require someone with integrity enough to strengthen her moral faculties. Is this you, Ms. Valdez?"

The back of my hand won't stop itching, but I won't

let myself move. Somehow I feel that to remain motion-less is to give myself an air of professionalism. "As you already know, I've worked with special children for over ten years. I've found that whatever a child's weaknesses, these shortcomings are often accompanied by equally powerful strengths. I have full confidence that I can help Isabella identify and develop these strengths."

"That sounds wonderful," Mrs. Evers says, gazing at her hand. "I think you could be the one we've been searching for. Don't you think so, Hubert?"

"I am more than satisfied." Mr. Evers stands, grinning. "You can begin tomorrow, but for now let's get you set-tled in."

Mrs. Evers glides over and takes my hand, coating my palm with her grandfather's ashes. I will myself not to look down. "Thank you for coming," she says. Her long, cool fingers bring to mind the faceless woman balancing on the trumeau.

"Come with me, miss," Robin says. She disappears into the hallway, and I follow her soon after.

On my way out, I hear the couple whispering. The only words that reach me are *virtues* and *fiend*.

Robin leads me down a dim hallway decorated with illuminated paintings. Each canvas houses an emaciated figure draped in tattered strips of gossamer. Wings made of human fingers spread out from their backs, and their ashen skin stretches tight over their bones like shrink-wrap. None of their faces have eyebrows or teeth or lips. The lights in the hallway flicker, all at once.

Robin is far ahead of me when she speaks, but she sounds close. Her voice carries in a way that reminds me of my mother's. "I can tell that whole wallet business ruffled your feathers, but don't let it bother you, miss. Mr. Evers is what some might call an eccentric, but he's a good man and a good employer. Have you ever had a boss who would lend you five hundred dollars so that you could help your son? Can't remember why my son needed the money, but it was important, I can tell you that much, miss. Don't give that wallet another thought."

By the time Robin finishes speaking, we're in a chamber saturated with prismatic color and the smell of bleach. A stained-glass window the length of my Hyundai dominates the west wall. The window depicts dozens of headless figures trekking through a stark landscape.

"Told you, didn't I?" Robin says, motioning to another eighty-four-inch, high-definition television on the opposite wall.

"It's a lovely room," I say.

"Oh yes. It's one of my favorites. In here, you almost feel yourself in a dream." Robin releases my luggage trolley. Then she opens and closes her hand again and again.

"If you need anything, miss, just give me a ring. My cell number is right there on the table. As for dinner, you're welcome to join Raul and me in the servants' hall. *Servants' hall* sounds so dreary, but I assure you, miss, it's quite well furnished and impeccably decorated. Of course, after such a long journey, I suspect you're not in the mood for much socializing. I can bring you your dinner, if you'd prefer."

"Thank you." I sit on the edge of my bed. "Maybe I will eat in here tonight. I'll join you for breakfast tomorrow."

"Very good, miss. I'll bring you your dinner as soon as possible."

Robin heads for the door, even faster now without the luggage trolley to slow her down.

"Robin," I say, "before you go, can you tell me anything about Isabella?"

The old woman sighs. "A very sweet girl. Very bright."

"In the letter Mr. Evers sent me, he mentioned there was an accident?"

"Yes." Robin rubs her hands together. "Mrs. Evers will explain. I shouldn't say any more before Mrs. Evers explains. What I can tell you, miss, is that you need to go into this with an open mind. But I shouldn't say any more. I'll return with your dinner soon, miss. Do you have any allergies?"

"Dairy. And you can call me Danna, if you'd like."

"Danna. That's a lovely name, miss. Danna."

Robin vanishes, and I finally scratch the back of my hand. A rash in the shape of a dog inflames my skin. When I was a girl, my father told me that God chattered constantly to mankind in the form of omens. What would my father see in this dog on my hand? I laugh a little, and lie on what could be a silk charmeuse blanket. After kicking off my shoes, I turn to the headless figures of stained glass on the west wall. Men, women, children. They're staggering, crawling through a desert of blackened trees and jagged stones. Some of the figures hold a skull in their hands. Maybe their own.

I roll over and face the enormous television. Before I can even turn on the TV, I drift into a white room without any windows or doors. I get the feeling that I've been here many times before. Dozens of fluorescent bulbs intersect on the ceiling, forming a labyrinth of light. Malformed beetles creep and buzz inside the bulbs. I can see their silhouettes through the thin glass.

A voice whispers from under a mound of white blankets on the hospital bed.

"What are you saying?" I ask.

"Fiend," the voice says. "Fiend."

"I don't know what you want."

A small gray hand slides out from under the blankets. I sit on the bed and hold the icy, withered flesh. Only now do I notice the holes in the walls. There are eyes everywhere, peeking at us, never blinking.

"Go away," I say.

"Fiend," the voice says, quivering.

When I bring the hand closer to me, I discover that the flesh ends at the wrist. Quickly, I search the mound of blankets, but I can't find the rest of him.

I open my mouth to ask, "Where are you?" But I can't get my lips to part.

The fluorescent bulbs flicker. The beetles hiss.

I stand, holding the severed hand close to my chest. I'd like to leave, but there are shards of glass glittering on the linoleum, and I still can't find any sign of a door. The eyes in the wall blink faster and faster. The little hand holds me tight.

The next moment, I'm lying on a silk blanket, with a tray of roast beef and asparagus salad on the table beside me. I sit up and inspect my body. Olive cardigan, navy skirt, braided belt. This is a real outfit of mine. I must be awake.

Yes, there's the stained-glass window. There's the eighty-four-inch, high-definition television.

I haven't had such a vivid hospital dream for months now.

It's still dark out, so I turn on the white pansy Tiffany-style lamp near my bed.

The roast beef is cold, but I don't mind. At this point, I would wolf down a shrimp cocktail or two, and shrimp taste like salty rubber bands.

I accidentally bite down on my fork when something or someone slams against the door of my room.

"Hello?" I say, getting out of bed.

The door handle moves up and down, slowly.

"Who's there?"

As soon as I approach the door, the brass handle stops moving and I hear a high-pitched giggle coming from outside the door. The laughter sounds artificial, like a cartoon character's. I look down and I'm still wearing the olive cardigan, navy skirt, braided belt.

I reach out and open the door.

Looking left and right, I can't see anyone except for the cadaverous, winged figures hovering in the paintings. The closest figure seems to be looking right at me. A thick, pink maggot dangles from his lipless mouth.

I glance around again. "Isabella? Isabella, are you here? I need to talk with you."

No one responds.

Despite the breakneck pounding of my heart, I know on a conscious level that I'm not in any real danger. Isabella is playing some kind of game with me. She's only a little girl.

Back in my room, I decide to put on my pajamas, and

I discover that my luggage trolley is empty. Did Isabella sneak in while I was asleep and . . . ? No. Just because Isabella knocked on my door doesn't mean she would take my possessions.

After taking a deep breath, I approach the mahogany dresser adorned with squares of stained-glass roses. Inside, I find my clothing folded neatly away. Robin must have done this after bringing in my dinner.

I dress in my cat pajamas, worried that I won't be able to fall back asleep. But as soon as I cocoon myself under the covers, I return to the hospital, searching for Bruno and finding only pieces.

———————

In the morning, I follow Robin up a spiral staircase with human faces carved into the stone walls. Robin reminds me again that the servants' hall is well furnished and impeccably decorated.

"Mr. Evers surprised us with a pool table about six months ago," Robin says. "It's regulation size with hand-sewn leather pockets. The oak was salvaged from nineteenth-century tobacco barns. In truth, miss, I'm not positive what a tobacco barn is, but it is nice having a piece of history in our little room."

"That sounds nice," I say.

The faces in the wall become increasingly malformed and contorted the higher we step. A man's eyes look in different directions while his lips push out farther than humanly possible. A child's bottom teeth grow upward like tusks, covering his eyes. A woman's enormous nose bends and enters one of her eye sockets.

At last, we come to the servants' hall, and as Robin promised, the place is not dreary in the least. Impressionist floral paintings cover the pale blue walls. Natural light spills in from four towering bow windows. The room is crowded with red oak chairs, a red oak dining table, and of course the tobacco-barn pool table.

"This is Raul," Robin says. "Raul, come say hello to Miss Danna."

Raul turns away from the pool table and gives me a little smile. He's dressed in dark jeans and a plaid shirt with rolled-up sleeves. My eyes wander for a moment to the foot-long knife on his belt.

"Hello," he says, shaking my hand. His skin feels calloused and cracked.

"It's nice to meet you," I say.

"You, too."

Raul returns to the pool table, and Robin sighs. "That man," she says. "Always the talkative one. You'll hear longer stories from the paintings on the walls."

I think of the gaunt figure outside my bedroom door,

with bulging yellow eyes and crooked teeth.

At the dining table, Robin serves us a breakfast of eggs royale and fresh strawberries. "I made a dairy-free hollandaise for you, miss. Can't say it tastes exactly the same as the traditional sauce, but it isn't an unpleasant commingling of flavors. If you don't like the hollandaise, you can be honest with me. I won't take offense."

I swallow a bite. "It's delicious. Thank you, Robin."

"I'm relieved to hear that, miss."

For a while, Robin studies my face in silence. "Please don't take this the wrong way, miss. But it looks as if you had some trouble sleeping last night? Not that you appear anything less than elegant. It's only, you seem as if sleep eluded you."

"This house will do that to you," Raul says, joining us at the table.

Robin nods. "I don't know if you've noticed this, miss, but there are a number of unsightly paintings and things in Stockton House. If you're susceptible, these images can work their way into your subconscious and generate nightmares. What works for me, miss, is to watch a number of comedy programs on the television right before bed. If you're unfamiliar with current television programs, I would be more than happy to recommend a number of very funny shows. They aren't Shakespeare, miss, but they will do the trick."

"I appreciate the concern," I say. "I think I'll be fine."

"Ah. Very good, miss." Robin finally takes her first bite of food. "I hope you'll let me know if you need any help during your stay. The house can spin you around and leave you dizzy, if you get my meaning, miss."

"There is something I was wondering about," I say. "Someone banged on my door last night and laughed."

Raul glances at me. "That was probably—"

"That's not for us to say, Raul," Robin says, pointing her fork in his direction. "We should let Mrs. Evers explain. Don't you think that would be for the best?"

"Yeah," Raul says, with his mouth full of strawberries. "I suppose so."

I look at Raul and then Robin. Neither of them will meet my eyes. "I'm only wondering if Isabella does this sort of thing often."

"Mrs. Evers will explain," Robin says. "I do hope the hollandaise sauce is to your liking, miss."

After breakfast, Robin leads me to a large room with ocean green walls and an old-fashioned chalkboard below a stained-glass window. The window depicts a hairless child standing at the top of an oak tree, raising his hands to the sun. Colossal bookshelves cover two of the four walls. A single tablet arm chair sits empty in the center of the room.

Robin waves her tiny hand at one of the walls. "The

room used to be red, but Mrs. Evers hopes the green will help promote a relaxed learning environment. I should have warned you earlier, miss, but Mrs. Evers prefers us not to wear red, orange, or yellow. A little here or there is fine, only Mrs. Evers worries about overstimulation and cognitive overload."

At this point, I notice that all the books with red, orange, or yellow spines are located high up on the bookshelves.

"I'll leave you here, miss. Mrs. Evers will be with you shortly. Don't hesitate to call me if you need anything."

"Thank you for being so helpful, Robin."

Robin's lips twitch in a momentary smile. "No thanks necessary. It's my job."

She speeds toward the door but freezes in the doorway. She turns around. "I do hope to see you for lunch, but if you're already gone by then, I want you to know it was a pleasure meeting you, miss. You seem a kind sort of person."

With that, the old woman is gone.

I sit at a Chippendale-style walnut desk in the front of the room. The rash on the back of my hand has devolved from a dog into an amoeba. While I'm waiting, I flip through the textbooks and workbooks stacked in front of me. One of the completed workbooks begins with small, neat handwriting, and by the end, the lettering is replaced with cryptic hieroglyphs, angular like broken glass. A maelstrom of doodles fill some of the pages. In the chaos, I make out a face impaled with nails and a severed arm holding tight to a branch.

"Oh good," Mrs. Evers says. "You're here." The woman's dressed in a muted blue cocoon dress, and she wears her dark hair in a loose braid over her shoulder. "I hope you're not too upset about our little wallet test. I'm sure it was terribly unprofessional of us, but Hubert thought it would be for the best. He can be so overprotective when it comes to his family. We didn't offend you too much?"

"No," I say, standing. "But if you have any further questions regarding my character, I do hope that you'll speak to me directly."

"Oh, of course." Mrs. Evers flows over and takes both my hands. "Thank you again for coming all this way. I'm sure you'll do Isabella a world of good."

"I'm looking forward to working with her."

Mrs. Evers releases my hands. "I was hoping we could begin now, but I'm afraid Isabella is hiding. She does this from time to time. There are so many nooks and crannies in this house. It may take me some time to find her."

"Would you like me to help look for her?"

"No, no." Mrs. Evers waves away the thought. "Bell usually won't come out unless I'm alone. I'll go find her and you stay here and prepare."

Mrs. Evers turns around and flutters away. She leaves a scent of lavender in her wake.

I remove a folder from my woven leather satchel, and I make sure that I have all the necessary assessment materials.

At this point, I spend a few minutes writing out my initial impressions of the family and the staff. I know little about Isabella herself for the time being, except that she broke her great-grandfather's urn and she banged on my door during the night. Is she sneaking off at any little opportunity, or is she being left unsupervised? As is sometimes the case with the affluent families I work for, Isabella might be feeling ignored by her parents. It's clear to me that Mr. and Mrs. Evers care for their daughter, but do they spend any quality time with her?

As these questions whirl around in my head, I draw the hairless, faceless woman from the trumeau. But I give her a face. I give her thin, pale lips with the weakest of smiles. Her eyes are dark and sunken.

Minutes pass. An hour? Eventually, I take out my phone and look through the photos from my cousin Isaac. Today, he's sent me a kitten in a Christmas sweater riding on the shell of a giant tortoise. He's also sent me an American bulldog dressed up as the Hamburglar. It's been about five years since Isaac started this tradition of texting me photos every morning, and he's only missed a handful of days. I should find a way to thank him properly. But what else can I do? What else can I say?

I message him another thank-you.

Finally, Mrs. Evers returns, and there's still no sign of Isabella.

"I'm so sorry for making you wait," Mrs. Evers says, stepping to the center of the room. "I finally found her inside a wardrobe in one of the guest rooms. Bell is a dear girl, but she does enjoy her little games, no matter the inconvenience they might impose on the rest of us." She releases a frail, breathy laugh. "Bell, sit down. It's time for your lessons."

I look to the doorway, but the girl doesn't appear.

Mrs. Evers faces the empty tablet arm chair beside her. "Bell, this is Ms. Valdez. Your new governess."

I look to the doorway again.

Mrs. Evers squeezes the fingers of her left hand with her right hand. "You can't see her, can you?"

"What?" I say.

"I was afraid you wouldn't. Most people can't." The woman looks down at her black wedge sandals. "You see, um. You see, Isabella passed away in February. It was an accident, and . . . I know what you must be thinking, Ms. Valdez. I know this is a peculiar sort of situation. But . . . but I assure you, Isabella is sitting right here in this chair.

I can see her clear as day." Mrs. Evers looks at me, and a beam of red light from the stained-glass window coats her face.

At this moment, my face and chest feel warm. The room around me seems fragile, as if any sudden movement would cause the whole scene to shatter.

"Mrs. Evers," I say. "I'm so sorry to hear that. I . . . I don't know what you expect me to do."

The woman squeezes one of her fingernails. "Please don't leave us. Please. We've had two prospective governesses sitting at that desk, and as soon as they learned the truth, they left us." Mrs. Evers trickles toward me and whispers, "Isabella isn't coping well with this new phase of her existence. A few months ago, she started breaking things. At first it was only a lamp or a vase every few weeks, but things are . . . escalating. Hubert and I both agree that what our daughter needs is structure. She needs to feel normal again. Please stay, Ms. Valdez. At least for a little while?"

"I don't think I'm qualified to—"

"All that we ask is that you give your lessons and speak to Bell as if she's one of your regular students. Please."

For a few moments, I look into the woman's dark, moist eyes.

I don't believe in ghosts, at least not the kind that would break vases or sit in a chair. But I know what it means to lose a child. Even if I can't help Isabella, maybe I can provide some comfort for Mrs. Evers, or point her in the direction of a therapist? At the very least, I should take some time to think things through before abandoning this woman.

"I can't make you any promises," I say. "But I'll stay for now."

"Oh, good." Mrs. Evers uses her finger to dab at a tear in the corner of her eye. "Ordinarily, Bell is unable to communicate in a traditional sense. Will this be a problem in regard to her education?"

"I . . . No."

"I'm so happy to hear that. Well, I'm sure Bell doesn't want her mother intruding in her classroom all day. I'll leave you two to your work."

Mrs. Evers walks out the door. And I'm sitting at my new desk, facing the green lounge chair with the tablet arm. The leaf-shaped clock on the far wall taps away the seconds.

What exactly am I doing here?

I came to this house to escape empty rooms.

The word *ARMADILLO* is written on the mahogany podium in gold letters, in elegant uncials. On top of the podium, a creature squirms, blinking at me with big brown eyes. Pale, bony plates cover his rounded skull. He's held down with wire, but he manages to reach out at me with his one good hand. His other shriveled arm is missing the hand.

The creature's good hand brushes against my arm. He blinks faster and faster.

"Is this really an armadillo?" I ask.

I search the white, bleach-scented room. A woman in a lab coat shoves a chicken into a wheezing pneumatic tube, which sucks the creature into the ceiling. Without looking, the woman reaches for another chicken on the pile. Are the chickens living or dead? I can't tell.

"Excuse me," I say. "I have a question about the armadillo?"

The woman ignores me.

On the other side of the room, a group of women and children stand perfectly still, facing a terrarium built into the wall.

I can feel the armadillo's thin fingers grazing my back.

One of the women in the crowd says, "Could you be quiet? We're trying to listen."

I try to look through the wall of people at the terrarium, but all I can make out is something writhing on the jagged stones.

"Quiet," the woman says.

"I can't hear them eat," a little girl says.

They all face me now, showing me their long, ashen faces. I turn away from the crowd, and the armadillo grips my neck and squeezes.

Only now do I hear myself. I'm screaming. I must have been screaming the whole time.

The armadillo opens his toothless maw and shrieks with me.

I open my eyes, coughing, with the creature's clammy fingers touching my face. No, these are my fingers. I sit up at the walnut desk and inspect my body. I'm still wearing the mustard cardigan, polka-dot skirt, leopard-print belt. I must be awake.

A glimmer of crimson light dances on the empty lounge chair in front of me. For an instant, I can see a face in the anarchic shimmer. She smiles an impish smile and then disappears.

"How is everything?" Mrs. Evers asks from the doorway.

I stand and straighten my cardigan. "It's fine. Everything's fine."

"Bell isn't causing you too much trouble, I hope?"

"No, not at all."

"Oh, good." Mrs. Evers squeezes the end of her loose braid. "Well. I'll see you both later."

"Mrs. Evers," I say, but she's already out the door.

I grip a piece of white chalk and consider writing my name on the board. The thought forces a feeble snicker out of me, but I shouldn't be laughing. An invisible flame heats up my face.

I stare at the lounge chair.

What if Mrs. Evers is right about Isabella? What if she bangs on doors and hides in wardrobes and wants to learn her times tables? What if Bruno's standing beside me in his Slimer pajamas, waiting for me to touch his ethereal face and say everything a mother should say?

But of course, Mrs. Evers is not right about Isabella.

The chair is empty.

I take out my phone and look at a possum dressed in a Victorian-style wedding gown.

At a little after one, Robin enters the classroom and beams in my direction. "You're still here, miss? You've decided to stay?"

"For now," I say. "To be honest, I . . . I'm not sure how much I can help here."

"Ah. That is something to consider, miss." The old woman leads me out the door and races down the hallway, peeking back at me from time to time. "I know this is only your first day on the job, but the whole house seems brighter since your arrival. Not two hours ago, I spotted Mrs. Evers walking in the garden. This might seem of little consequence to you, miss, but I assure you, what I witnessed was a small miracle. Mrs. Evers hasn't left the house for eighty-four days. When she was out in the garden, it was disheartening to see her stepping on the perennials without any consideration of Raul's hard work. But at least she was outside, miss. At least she was smiling."

During our trek through the labyrinthine hallways, we pass by a painting of an angel, her scabrous face ripped apart as if by a claw. Spiral strips of hemp flesh dangle over her throat. Maybe the sight should disturb me, but all I feel is relief that at least one monster in this house has been slain. The thought is ridiculous.

We turn another corner, and at the end of the corridor sits a giant rodent with eyes like a tarsier. A bizarre-sounding gasp escapes my throat.

Without even pausing for a moment, Robin rushes forward and grabs the rodent by the head. "No need to worry, miss. It's a stuffed animal. Isabella had a strong fascination with capybaras and other rodents. The bigger the better was her motto, it seemed to me. Mrs. Evers has no love for rats and the like, but she did everything she could to support Isabella's interests. No mother is perfect, myself included, but Mrs. Evers did adore that little girl." Robin's voice cracks, and her body slows a little. "I hope you don't mind a little detour, miss."

In a minute or two, we enter a messy bedroom with

blue-gray walls and a massive picture window that looks out into the back garden. Decorating the ceiling are intricate line drawings of porcupines, flying squirrels, and other furry creatures. The bed is unmade.

A cottage-style playhouse sits at the end of the room, complete with gingerbread trim and wooden shutters and a railed porch. A stuffed rat stares at me from one of the flower boxes, nestled in a bed of artificial lavender.

"I'll be right back, miss," Robin says. "We'll be enjoying our lunch before we know it."

The old woman carefully navigates an obstacle course of open books and oversized pencils and serpentine parades of plastic animals. After patting the capybara on the head, Robin places the toy in the other flower box.

"She used to say they were her guards," Robin says, motioning to the capybara. "She said her creatures would come alive at night and speak with her. Isabella had a vivid imagination, miss. She was a special girl."

Just as Robin predicted, I'm enjoying my lunch before I know it. Robin serves us watermelon gazpacho and pan-seared grouper with lemon and capers.

"I'll ask you, miss," Robin says, holding her empty fork near her face. "What other boss would invite his domestic staff to enjoy the same meals as his own family? Say what you will about Mr. Evers, but he's no Scrooge. Did I ever tell you about the time he lent me five hundred dollars so that I could help my son? I think I did. Are you enjoying your lunch, miss? You can be honest with me."

"It's delicious," I say.

A moment later, Raul enters, bringing with him the scents of fresh-cut grass and manure. A thin cut travels up his arm like a snake.

"Are you all right?" I say.

"Oh, this?" Raul raises his arm. "I had a disagreement with a rosebush. Things got heated, but we've worked out our differences."

"That's good to hear. You should never go to bed angry."

"Raul, don't be silly." Robin stabs at the nonsense with her fork. "Anyway, have you heard the good news? Miss Danna has decided to stay with us."

"Nothing's definite yet," I say. "I'm here for now, but . . . I came here to teach. I don't know if—"

"Isabella might still be with us," Robin says, balancing a single caper on her fork. "In truth, I haven't seen any apparitions in Stockton myself, miss, but Mrs. Evers seems quite sure of such a presence. Who are we to say, one way or the other?" She swallows the caper. "I don't know if I've told you this, miss, but my mother died twelve years ago from extrahepatic bile duct cancer. A rare disease to take a rare woman. She competed in two Olympic Games. Did I ever mention that? Anyway, the night she died, I woke up at 1:05, and who did I see sitting on the end of my bed, dressed in a straw hat and muumuu? My mother, only her eyes were bigger than usual. I asked her what she was doing in my room, and she opened her mouth, but nothing came out. My mother was always quite a chatterbox, miss, so I knew something was wrong. Suddenly, the room smelled like jasmine. Before I could say anything else, my mother disappeared. I learned later that she had passed away at 12:57 that night. Now, as I said, I haven't seen Isabella in an incorporeal form, but I wouldn't dismiss Mrs. Evers's claim willy-nilly. There are more things in heaven and earth, Horatio, as they say."

We eat in silence for a few moments. The rash on the back of my hand has devolved from an amoeba into a tiny red dot.

Raul clears his throat and says, "Sometimes I hear voices in the hedge. Always near the Atrocities."

Robin points her knife at the gardener. "Be serious, Raul."

"I am," he says, staring at his gazpacho. "The sound is so quiet, though, I'm never sure what I'm hearing. It could be my mind is misinterpreting the wind in the leaves."

"Ah," Robin says. "Might be we'll never find out the truth about Isabella, but it breaks my heart to think of such a sweet girl trapped here in the physical realm. I'll ask you, miss, if an innocent girl doesn't deserve her time in heaven, then who does? On numerous occasions, I've told Mrs. Evers about the mediums from the television. I'm sure there are countless frauds out there, but these particular psychics are most impressive, I can tell you that much, miss. I'm confident Mr. Evers could hire one of these women to fly here and help poor Isabella, but Mrs. Evers says that Isabella isn't ready to cross over. I suppose Mrs. Evers knows best when it comes to her own daughter."

I can't think of how to respond to Robin's words, so I eat the cold, dead grouper in silence.

————————

Isabella refuses to join us in the classroom this afternoon, so Mrs. Evers takes me by the hand and leads me to the garden behind the house. Outside, we travel a pebble-mosaic walkway with an intricate pattern of white flowers and human-faced insects.

"This way," she says. Her hand feels small and cold.

We pass through a number of rose-covered arches before coming to an open area bursting with creeping phlox, anise hyssops, and other flowers in shades of red and purple. Prismatic butterflies dance across the sky and quiver over glistening petals.

Mrs. Evers pulls me toward a wrought-iron bench with a spiral design. A wide, metal eye nests in the center of each spiral. Nearby, a marble warrior rides a human-faced bumblebee, raising an elongated arm, pointing a spear at the sky. Water rushes from the tip of his weapon into the fountain's octagonal base.

Mrs. Evers motions for me to sit on the bench, but she doesn't join me. Instead, she stands in front of the fountain, biting at a fingernail. A monarch butterfly hovers near her braided bun.

"I'm so sorry for the inconvenience," Mrs. Evers says. "Ordinarily, Bell will follow me when I find her. But right now, she refuses to leave the bench."

"I don't mind," I say. "It's beautiful out here."

"It is. Yes."

At the far end of the garden, Raul stabs at the ground with his knife, again and again. He wipes his face with a red handkerchief. For a moment, the fabric appears like an open gash across his neck.

"Well," Mrs. Ever says, "I hate to lock myself inside on such a beautiful day, but I have work to do. I'll leave you to your lessons."

She heads for the mosaic path, but I say, "Wait. Mrs. Evers. Could I speak with you for a moment?"

The woman faces me again, her pale eyes narrowing in the sunlight. "Yes?"

"Mrs. Evers, I want you to know . . . If you ever need someone to talk to, I'm here. I'm no therapist, but I know what it's like to lose a child."

"I haven't lost her," Mrs. Ever says, the words rushing out of her like a savage river. "She's sitting right beside you, clear as day." She touches the side of her face with curled fingers. "But I . . . I know what you mean. Things have certainly changed between Bell and me. Much has been . . . lost."

"I'm so sorry."

Mrs. Evers sits at the edge of the fountain, and I join her. She dips a fingertip into the water and circles a cerulean petal. "She opens her mouth sometimes, as if to speak to me. But she can't. I'm sure it's terribly frustrating for her. She can sometimes nod yes and shake her head no, but that seems to be the extent of her abilities. I've tried teaching her some sign language. I bought a book. But her fingers, they seem stuck together like a doll's. She can't . . ."

Mrs. Evers pushes the petal into the water, and I can hear Raul stabbing at the ground again. He sounds closer to us now.

I place my hand on Mrs. Evers's back, but only for a moment.

"I wish Bell would leave the garden." She stands and faces the bench. "Come inside, Bell. Please?"

The fountain alone gurgles a cryptic reply.

Mrs. Evers speaks again, too quietly for me to hear, and walks away without another glance in my direction.

I sit at the bench, in the cool shadow of a jacaranda tree. My woven satchel leans against my ankle, but I left all my folders back in the classroom. I kick off my shoes. An electric blue butterfly spirals from above onto my foot and lies flat on my flesh. No. That's only a petal.

I look up, and a creature with a long hairy face scrambles out of the fountain. The giant guinea pig rushes in my direction, dragging a wet, wilted tutu under its belly. I know I should run, but my body freezes. A little voice whispers that this is the stuffed animal from the hallway come to life.

Out of nowhere, Raul materializes and grabs a pink harness on the creature's back.

"How is it that you keep escaping?" the gardener asks, and then looks at me. "I have a sneaking suspicion that she's learned how to pick locks."

"Maybe she's training to become an escape artist?"

"Maybe." The gardener's grin fades a little. "Honestly, though, I think she's looking for Isabella. The two of them were close. As close as a girl and her pet capybara can get, anyway."

Raul releases his grip on the harness as the creature grazes on the grass. She chirps with glee and wiggles her tiny ears.

"Can I pet her?" I ask.

"She's been a bit bitey lately. Stay away from her face, though, and you'll be fine."

"Never mind."

For a short time, we watch the capybara in silence. Her tutu dries out in the sun and expands like a blooming pink flower.

"I suppose I should get her back to the enclosure," Raul says. "Come on, Princess."

We say goodbye, and Raul jogs toward the side of the house, weaving around tufts of scarlet monkeyflowers and heartleaf milkweeds. The rodent trots along beside him, warbling away. I watch them until they become smears of earth-tone colors in the distance.

I take a deep breath. Another.

Years ago, I wasn't the kind of person who would sit and search the air for butterflies and wiggle her toes in the soft grass. But here I am. After years of practice, these halcyon moments in a natural setting feel almost natural. Of course I still suffer a faint nausea of guilt, like a cat's gentle kneading on my stomach. Why should I enjoy the sun on my skin when Bruno and Isabella can't?

I take another deep breath.

Then I reach out and touch the air beside me on the bench, but I don't feel a thing.

I skip dinner because of a headache that brings to mind two beetles hugging the backs of my eyes with strong, wiry legs. In my room, Robin serves me a cup of soup with pink spirals floating on the surface. I thank her, and as soon as she's gone, I pour the noodles into the toilet. I can't have food near me right now. Even the faint doughy smell still clinging to the air is getting to me.

In bed, I arrange five novels on the silk charmeuse blanket. I inspect the covers carefully, as if I'm reading Tarot cards for my future. One illustration shows a ring of moss-coated standing stones with a hole in the center. There's a man in a straw hat attempting to pull himself out of the darkness, or is he lowering himself inside? Another illustration shows a woman peering through a window marred with spidery cracks. Her nude body appears shattered to pieces. Why is she smiling?

Before I can decide on a book, I'm sliding into a room with jaundiced walls and oxidized metal beds. Flecks of glittering dust swirl in the air like a swarm of gnats, only to settle on the tile floor a moment later.

The mouths in the walls open and close, open and close. They reveal black, broken teeth that remind me of a shelf in my old house decorated with volcanic glass. Someone collected these shimmering rocks. I can't remember who.

The mouths wheeze and groan. Grublike tongues poke out, quivering, licking the chapped lips. I can tell the mouths are hungry, but there isn't a food tray to be seen. The mouths moan even louder, like dying animals. At this point, I begin pulling the brass handles on the floor tiles, opening little doors. One door reveals a dark tunnel that blasts a stream of sour air into my face. This must lead to a mountain of used syringes and bloody bandages and discarded body parts down below the hospital. For a moment, I can see pale serpents interlacing their bodies throughout the refuse. Their humanlike faces grin up at me.

Another opening in the floor shows me a man in a gray checked suit sitting on the toilet.

"I'm so sorry," I say, and as soon as I speak, the man's whole body lurches as if struck by lightning. He can obviously hear me, but he makes no attempt to acknowledge my apology. His downcast eyes don't shift from the fishing magazine on his lap. He licks his finger and flips past page after page of decomposing swordfish and sharks and mackerels. The fish stare up at me with wide open eyes and wide open mouths. Maybe I shouldn't be opening random doors in the floor, but that's no excuse for this man to ignore my existence.

"I said I'm sorry."

The man's body lurches again, only this time he falls over.

His body flounders on the grimy floor, and sparkling dust erupts from his mouth. I shut the door quickly as my heart squirms in my chest.

In the next floor compartment, I find a small shoebox packed with hamburger meat. Smiling, I scoop up two handfuls and approach the nearest mouth in the wall.

"Here you go," I say, keeping my hand flat, as if I'm feeding one of my cousin's horses.

He gulps down the raw meat with a sort of fierce desperation. Soon, grunts of pleasure replace his agonized moans. When I run out of hamburger, his slimy tongue wiggles on my palm, searching for more.

"That's enough for now," I say.

The mouth clacks his fractured teeth at me in annoyance.

I feed another, and another. In time, the satiated mouths begin singing in guttural, sepulchral tones. I can feel the music on my skin, mimicking the sensation of a hot bath after a late-night walk. My heart twirls. The shimmering blue dust bounces on the floor.

A man in a white lab coat seems to materialize out of nowhere, but I know that can't be true. He snaps his fingers at the mouths, quieting them. Clusters of pink scabs form a Rorschach test on his wide forehead. In the dry crust of flesh, I see two dogs facing each other, baring their teeth.

"We need you on the table," the man says.

"I can't right now," I say. "Some of them are still hungry."

"They're not your concern." The man's voice sounds gentle, but I can see the grimace behind his diaphanous surgical mask. Flakes of skin detach from his face and drift to the floor like roseate snow. The Rorschach test now shows two old men with their heads twisted completely around. They reach for each other, but their bonelike fingers don't quite touch.

"Please lie down," the doctor says, pointing to the nearest bed with a scalpel. I have a sudden feeling that he's cut me before. And I'm afraid that he cut a piece out of me that I needed.

Taking a step back, I say, "I need to reschedule this procedure."

The man shakes his head, causing the Rorschach test to shift again. This time, I don't see a picture. I see only flesh, scabrous and peeling. "We can't wait anymore," he says, pulling me by the wrist. Only now do I notice that my hands are covered with blood from the hamburger meat. I hold my free hand as far away from the rest of my body as possible.

"I need to feed them," I say. "Let me go!"

But there is no escape from the man's marble fingers. Soon, he lifts me high above his head and slams me onto the metal table. The room trembles. Pale serpents rise from the floor, grinning with their human lips, and they interlace their bodies throughout my own limbs.

The mouths in the wall join me in a chorus of screams.

When I wake up, I can feel the blood, thick and slippery, coating my entire body. No, this is only sweat. The moonlight pushing through the stained-glass desertscape gives my skin a faint indigo glow.

I sit up in bed and inspect my body. I'm still wearing the pajamas with swing-dancing Maine Coons and trumpet-playing Scottish Folds. I must be awake.

When someone or something knocks on my door, my heart lurches like the startled man on the toilet. I imagine the doctor bursting into my room, pointing his scalpel at my face, his forehead crumbling. No, I'm awake now. This is real.

As I begin wriggling off the bed, my head feels studded with tacks.

"Hello?" I say.

The response comes in the form of a shrill giggle. Someone hammers on my door again, and I know I should hurry so the culprit doesn't have time to escape. But for a few moments, I stand frozen in the darkness, hugging my torso. I imagine a girl with big brown eyes and an impish smile. A crown of lavender flowers sits askew on her dark curls, and I can see through her phosphorescent face. There's a gaping wound on her chest that will never stop bleeding.

I open the door.

Instead of a girl, I find a small mound of squirming black rats. Another piercing cackle echoes in the hallway, but this one sounds faraway. I shut the door, and as I hurry in the opposite direction, I accidentally slam my knee into the bedside table. "Shit, shit, shit."

After turning on the Tiffany-style lamp, I grab my phone and activate the flashlight app. My heart won't stop throwing itself against my chest, like some crazed caged animal. With the door barely ajar, I shine a slice of light onto the rodents outside. This time, they're not writhing and flicking their tails. This time, they're only toys. They sit one on top of the other, some of the rats upside down, forming a chaotic pyramid. Their beady black eyes twinkle in the light of my phone.

I remember crawling across the orange-and-brown shag carpeting of my parents' bedroom. I remember meowing, and my parents would say, "Go to bed, baby." And I would say, "I'm not a baby. I'm a kitten." Sometimes, I would look over at the piles of laundry on their floor, and the shirts and pants seemed to wiggle slightly in the darkness, as if alive. The sight of the dancing laundry never bothered me, because even as a child I knew this was only a trick of the light. A trick of my mind.

After toppling the plastic rats with a gentle kick, I scan the hallway.

"Hello?" I say again.

Cacophonous barks of laughter lead me limping away from my doorway. I glance back once, to make sure the rats are still only toys. They are.

I move on. Brass fixtures perch above the hall paintings like slumbering birds, irradiating the angels with amber light. Eventually I come across one such painted figure with blood overflowing from her mouth and dripping down her bony chin. When I get closer, I can tell from the scent that the blood is actually ketchup. Farther down the hall, there's an angel with ketchup covering her eyes, bloody tears running down her hollow cheeks.

Someone in this house is playing a sick game, and I need to find out who. Whoever this person is may have convinced Mrs. Evers that Isabella is a ghost. This needs to end now. For my sake, and for Mrs. Evers's. With these thoughts swimming in my tack-studded mind, I move on, limping, shining my Android into the blackness ahead.

I follow the path of hemorrhaging angels to a pair of white faces resting on the terracotta floor. Someone seems to have shattered the ceramic faces and pieced them back together haphazardly. Looking closer, I notice that the man's nose is upside down. And the woman's missing eye is sitting on the man's forehead.

Haven't I seen these faces before?

Yes, these are the scowling visages from the urns on the mantelpiece. Moving forward, I notice what could be a trail of dust, or human ashes. I follow this sinuous trail through narrow corridors lined with lace-covered windows. The ashes lead me to another ceramic face on the floor. This one is missing both eyes, and ketchup covers her lips and cheeks. A stuffed porcupine wears the ceramic face like a mask.

"Hello?" I say, to the empty hall.

Minutes later, I come to a doorway. I suppose part of me knew the ashes would deliver me here, to Isabella's room. Black-light tubes on the ceiling shine on the drawings of squirrels and gophers and beavers. The animals glimmer in fluorescent violet and deep blue. I search for a light switch near the doorway, but I can't find one.

Suddenly, I hear a small voice whispering in the direction of the miniature cottage. I point my light at the playhouse, but I can't see anyone. The little door is closed.

"Who's there?" I ask.

The only response is more whispering and half-suppressed giggles.

I make my way across the room, careful not to touch any of the books or plastic animals, as if they might be booby-trapped. Once, I almost slip on an oversized pencil, and I gasp overdramatically. Angry-looking symbols ooze down the playhouse door, written in ketchup.

As I step closer, a memory drifts inside me of my father sniffing the floorboards, saying, "It smells like death down there." And then I followed him outside and watched as he slowly unscrewed the metal vent of the crawlspace. I pictured a child lying under the house, her arms crossed over her chest, her whole body covered with worms. What my father pulled out was a stiff-legged possum.

What I find in the playhouse is a slight figure with a mouse-print blanket draped over her body like some cartoon ghost. She sits facing a wooden table topped with brightly colored cups. The top of a Heinz bottle pokes out of a baroque teapot.

"Hello?" I say.

The figure titters but stays perfectly still.

Part of me hopes there's a real human being under that blanket, and an equally powerful part of me hopes there isn't.

I pinch the blanket between two fingers and lift.

Mrs. Evers snorts with laughter, her hands coated with ashes, her hair decorated with sticks and purple flowers. She's dressed in a tattered white sleepshirt, hugging a stuffed capybara close to her chest.

A cold, invisible hand wraps around me and squeezes.

"Mrs. Evers," I say. I know I should say more, but the words won't come.

"You should see your face!" she says, her voice high and unnatural, like a cartoon bird's. "Go look in the mirror!"

"Mrs. Evers, what are you doing in here?" Even as I'm speaking, I feel as if my body is running on automatic. My consciousness is a ball of static, hovering somewhere above my head, near the shingled roof of the cottage.

The woman grips my wrist with frozen fingers. Somehow, every lamp in the bedroom flares into brilliance as soon as she exits the playhouse. She drags me to a mirror on the wall, decorated with brass calla lilies.

"Look," Mrs. Evers says. "Look!"

In the grainy reflection, I appear as a lone figure lost in a fog. The woman's wan face stares silently ahead with dark, sunken eyes. Dewdrops of sweat linger on her forehead. I can still feel my consciousness orbiting my body, not quite touching my skin, not quite accepting that the woman in the mirror is definitely me.

After what could be a moment or a minute, I break free from my gaze. And I find Mrs. Evers sitting cross-legged on the floor, chattering into the furry ear of the stuffed capybara.

"Why did you do this?" I ask.

Without looking at me, she says, "I was just playing."

I need answers from Mrs. Evers, but she's obviously in

no state to give them. Without warning, my consciousness and my body collide, merging again. I can feel the
last of my energy flowing from my feet, like water escaping a cracked fish tank. At any moment, the fissure could
expand and everything could burst.

"We need to get you back to your room," I say.

Mrs. Evers laughs and grins at me with all her teeth.
She says, "This is my room."

I suppose I should have suspected this, after everything Mrs. Evers has shown me tonight. Here she is, playing in Isabella's room. She's whispering to her daughter's
stuffed animal. She's using the high-pitched voice of a
child.

"We should go talk to Mr. Evers," I say, holding out my
hand to the small woman.

"I want to sleep here," Mrs. Evers says. "Will you tuck
me in?"

Before I have time to reply, Mrs. Evers stands and
rushes over to the four-poster bed. For a while, she crawls
in circles under the quilt like an animal searching for
food. Finally she pokes her head and arms out near the
pillows. In her left hand, she's holding a small remote that
she uses to turn off the lamps.

I tuck her in, the way I haven't tucked in anyone for
seven years. I pluck the twigs and flowers out of her hair,
and I place them carefully on the bedside table.

She says, "Did you know most types of mice don't need to drink water? It's true. You can look in my book if you don't believe me."

"I believe you," I say.

Mrs. Evers closes her eyes. Soon, she begins snoring.

I need to speak with Mr. Evers, of course, but that can wait until tomorrow. For now, I collapse onto a teal bean-bag and look up at the bed for as long as possible. Moments or minutes pass. As soon as I close my eyes, I lose myself in a chimerical fog. Hazy, slender figures appear before me, but when I reach out to touch them, they dissipate, leaving me lost and alone.

———————

When the fog finally clears, I find myself suffused in sunlight, back in my own bed. How did I get here? A vague memory scratches at my mind of Mrs. Evers holding my hand, towing me through the byzantine path to my room. She whispered to me in the dark hallways, too quiet for me to hear. She squeezed my hand gently.

While lying in bed, I look through the photos from Isaac. Today, he's sent me a baby dressed up as Colonel Sanders. He's also sent me a lion cuddling with a miniature dachshund.

A little voice tells me to turn off my phone and keep sleeping, but a little voice always tells me to keep sleeping.

I dress in a vermillion cardigan, a chartreuse floral dress, and a thin black belt. In the mirror, my clothes give off a faint aura of cheerfulness and optimism. I will myself to absorb this energy, as if through osmosis, but I don't feel any different.

On my way to the servants' hall, I find no scattered ashes or shattered faces or bleeding angels. An ambiguous floral fragrance lingers in the air, intermingled with the acrid smell of bleach. Lace curtains slump lifeless over closed windows.

Before long, Robin materializes at the end of a narrow corridor. Today she's wearing a gray dress and a muslin apron embroidered with pale blue eggs.

"Hello, miss," she says. "I was just on my way to your room. I thought you might want an escort to breakfast."

"I need to speak with Mr. Evers," I say. "Can you take me to him?"

"Ah," she says, smoothing her apron with both hands. "Are you sure you wouldn't rather have breakfast first, miss? I made almond-crusted French toast with fresh berries and sliced bananas. I made sure to use almond milk for your toast, miss."

"I appreciate that, Robin, but I need to see Mr. Evers now."

The housekeeper rubs her hands together. "I'm sure he'd be happy to see you, only he's currently at work in his studio and he doesn't like to be disturbed."

"This is important."

Robin nods. "Of course, miss."

For a moment, she stares at the floor in silence. Then she pulls a smartphone from her apron pocket and makes a call.

"Ms. Valdez would like to see you, sir." Her eyes widen. "Oh? I will, sir." She lowers the phone and looks me in the eyes. "He says he'll see you now, miss. He says he's expecting you. I'll show you the way."

Without another word, Robin twirls and scurries away.

In an unfamiliar hallway, she slows a little and says, "Did I ever tell you that Mr. Evers surprised us with these smartphones about two months ago? They have five-inch screens, twenty-three-megapixel cameras, and three gigabytes of RAM. In truth, miss, I'm not positive what megapixels and RAM are, but Mr. Evers implied that the specifications are state-of-the-art."

We come to a pallid wooden door carved with a motif of climbing vines. Plump eyes dangle from the vines like grapes. After knocking three times, Robin opens the door and ushers me inside. Instantly, the stench of linseed oil and turpentine hits my face. The faintest aroma of coffee manages to touch me through the stink.

"Come in, Ms. Valdez," Mr. Evers says, over to my right.

But I can't take my eyes off the clay statue in front of me. The sculpture depicts a maelstrom of elongated limbs and hairless faces. In my imagination, the whirlpool of flesh swirls around a murky vortex. The lipless mouths open wider, wider.

"It's an intriguing piece, isn't it?" Mr. Evers says.

Breaking free from the vision, I turn to Mr. Evers. He's dressed in blue jeans and a beige smock freckled with color. Painted on his forehead is an amorphous, crimson eye surrounded by spirals.

He taps the eye with the tip of a black paintbrush and says, "You'll have to forgive my little absurdities. My grandfather wore a similar symbol while he painted, and I haven't the heart to break from tradition. But you aren't here to muse over my family's idiosyncrasies. Please sit down." He motions to a velvet armchair positioned on a white muslin backdrop.

On my way to the chair, I lock eyes with the angel on the nearest easel. She resembles the paintings from the hallway, with her wings comprised of human fingers and toes. But unlike her exsanguinous cousins, her face exudes a startling sense of vitality, as if she might reach out at any moment. One pleading eye stares ahead while the other commingles with her ear. Her nose bends to the side, and the line of her frown travels down her chin at a diagonal. If not for the asymmetry of her face, she would be beautiful.

Angels like her float on the walls, gripping skulls and flowers, writhing their bodies in transparent robes. I know these creatures are only paintings, but here on the velvet armchair, I feel as if I'm on display in a crowded room. Soft boxes point at me without emitting any light.

"I know why you're here," Mr. Evers says, grinning at me from across the room. "Last night you caught a glimpse or two of the phantom haunting my wife's psyche. And now you're here to ascertain whether or not my Molly is being cared for." He polishes his speckled glasses with a red hand-kerchief. "Firstly, I truly appreciate your concern for my family's well-being. You are, it turns out, the kind, empathetic person we all hoped you would be. Secondly, you can put your worries to rest as far as my wife is concerned. She has at her disposal a team of mental health professionals, including a psychiatrist, a psychologist, etcetera, etcetera. The phantom in my wife's mind may wreak havoc on certain household items, but the doctors assure me that Molly herself is in no physical danger."

"Mr. Evers, you should have told me all this during our initial communications."

He takes a few steps closer to me and clears his throat. Behind him, a clay man trapped in the cyclone of bodies glares at me with eyes full of spirals. "I suppose you're right," Mr. Evers says. "My wife's episodes have occurred so infrequently the past few months, I had hoped not to burden you with them. But your frustrations with me are not unfounded. You'll have to forgive me my discretion."

I stand, and I can feel Mr. Evers's eyes on my legs. "I'm sorry for your loss, and I wish I could help your wife, but I can't."

"There you're wrong," he says, shifting his gaze to my face. "We're faced with two possible versions of reality, and in either case your presence would only benefit my family. In one reality, the doctors are correct and Molly is suffering a shattered psyche. Her desire to connect with Isabella and do right by her has manifested as a sort of psychological possession. And since Molly believes that Isabella's poltergeistlike outbursts can be tempered with your influence, then her faith in you will make this so."

He takes a deep breath. "And now let us slip into the other reality where Molly is correct, and Isabella has crossed the veil back to the world. You might see this possibility as beyond the realm of rationality, but I am not what you'd call a rational man. From an early age, I've rooted myself in spiritual mysteries and esoteric realms.

True, I haven't witnessed any phantoms walking the halls, but I'm not going to discount the possibility." He waves the paintbrush in my direction. "In the case of a true haunting, we would still need you. When Isabella was alive, she was a defiant child, and easy to anger. I'm afraid her temperament has only intensified since her passing. She's destroyed priceless heirlooms and family death masks. Of course, I love Isabella, and I want what's best for her, even now. And what she requires is structure and education, provided by a feminine role model who won't coddle her or indulge her every whim. My wife is an angel, but she isn't the one to take up this mantle." Mr. Evers cuts at the air with his paintbrush. "So there we have it, Ms. Valdez. I wish I could tell you which direction the truth lies, but unfortunately I'm as much in the dark as you are."

At this point, Mr. Evers stops and stares at me, waiting. My vision pushes past him to an angel on the wall, reaching for me with crooked, pale fingers. Her one eye peeks at me through her short bangs.

"I'm afraid I'm not qualified to help you," I say. "I'm sorry, but I'm going home."

"Very well," he says, and lets out a soft sigh. "I hope you—"

Mr. Evers never finishes his sentence because we're interrupted by a giant rodent in a pink tutu. The creature scampers through the open door and sniffs at the pungent air. For a few long moments, Mr. Evers glares at the capybara in silence, his arms crossed over his chest.

"Hello, Princess," I say, suddenly remembering the creature's name.

After glancing at me, Princess takes off in a flurry of copper fur. She gallops around the studio, emitting low clicking noises, knocking over easels and a metal bucket full of radishes and carrots and parsnips. Mr. Evers holds the screen of his phone close to his face. He whispers in rough consonants.

Eventually, Princess hops up onto a cushioned window seat and lazes in a shaft of powder blue light. From where I'm standing, she looks like a hulking loaf of bread. I feel a faint urge to curl up beside her and sleep.

"I apologize for the commotion," Mr. Evers says. "This is unacceptable."

"It's fine," I say.

I'm still standing on the white backdrop, frozen, as if posing for a photograph. Maybe I'm worried that any sudden movement will wake Princess and result in another minor rampage. For now, I decide to return to the chair and wait.

Moments later, Raul hastens into the room, his face and arms shiny with sweat. His serrated blade, smeared with black mud, dangles at his side.

"Animals belong outside, Mr. Guzman," Mr. Evers says, in a hushed yet hard tone. "Stockton House may no longer bear the responsibilities of a church, but it is still a sacred space."

"I'm sorry, sir," Raul says, approaching the slumbering rodent. "I don't know how she keeps escaping. I can't find any weaknesses in the enclosure."

Mr. Evers frowns at the gardener's back for a moment and then sighs. "Forgive me if I sounded churlish, Raul. I do trust your judgment in these matters."

"There's nothing to forgive, sir. I'll check the enclosure again and see what I can find." He pats the rodent on the back. "Come on, Princess."

Princess hops off the floral-print cushion and yawns, showing off her long beaver teeth. She scampers behind Raul as he heads for the door. Only now does the gardener seem to notice me. He smiles in my direction and I give a little wave in reply.

With the creature gone, Mr. Evers restores the toppled easels and the upturned bucket. Every step, every motion seems strained, as if he's moving in slow motion. He says, "I would send the cursed animal away, but Molly has lost enough already."

"I should go," I say, standing again.

"Yes, of course," Mr. Evers says, and he shakes my hand with a trembling palm. "Goodbye, Ms. Valdez."

"Goodbye."

Once I pass the tangle of pasty corpses, Mr. Evers clears his throat. He says, "Have you . . . seen her?"

I turn around. "What?"

"Have you seen my daughter? Her spirit?"

"No." The word seems to hover in the air between us, like one of the grotesque angels. I don't want to end our conversation like this, but what more can I say? What more can I do for this man?

Mr. Evers turns away, and I do the same.

On the trek back to my room, I'm forced to sit on the floor, with my back against the wall. I feel as if an invisible hand has grabbed hold of my body and spun me around and around.

I take a deep breath. Another.

Soon, when the dizziness passes, I spot a broken piece of ceramic beside me. I pick up the white fragment, which depicts a closed eye and a winged eyebrow.

"Are you well, miss?" Robin says, appearing at my side. "Should I call for the doctor?"

"No," I say, dropping the ceramic shard. "I get dizzy sometimes, but it's only an inner ear thing. I'm fine."

The old woman squeezes her hands together. "Are you

quite sure, miss? You complained of a headache last night, and you still seem a little flushed. I have a wide selection of over-the-counter and prescription medications at the ready if you'd rather bypass the doctor visit."

"I'm fine, really."

To prove my point, I stand and straighten my cardigan. "Will you be joining us for breakfast now, miss?"

"I just quit, so maybe I should pack up and go."

"Oh no, miss. Eat first, and then Raul can drive you back to town. He has a small utility vehicle that can navigate the twists and turns of the hedge. I was somewhat hesitant to ride in such a vehicle, but I'll tell you, miss, it's not as harrowing as it seems. Raul drives like a snail, and the UTV has cushioned seats and integrated cup holders."

If Raul had one of these vehicles when I first arrived, why didn't he drive me through the maze? Was this another absurd test, like the lost wallet? I could ask Robin or Raul if they know anything about this, but I suppose the answer doesn't matter anymore.

We walk side by side, and somehow Robin suppresses her natural inclination to surge ahead. I can still feel the grip of the invisible hand around my body, shaking me a little from time to time. I focus on the mosaic floor streaming toward my feet.

During breakfast, the theme song from *Who's the Boss*

blares from under the dining table, and Robin jumps up from her chair. Into her phone, she says, "Hello, Mrs. Evers. Ah. Yes, I'll tell her." When she hangs up, she says, "That was Mrs. Evers, miss. She wants you to meet her in your bedroom." She sighs, still standing, holding the phone in her hand. "I should tell you, miss. Mrs. Evers is not in her right mind. I spoke with her early this morning, and she talked all sorts of nonsense. I knew that Mrs. Evers was sick with grief, but now she seems away with the fairies, as they say. In truth, miss, she frightened me, and I could understand if you'd rather not speak with her alone. I'm confident Mr. Evers would be happy to accompany you, or I could go with you myself. Or would you rather not speak with Mrs. Evers at all?"

"I'm happy to talk with her," I say. "I'll be fine alone."

"Ah." Robin gives me her phone number for the second time. "Call me if you need anything," she says, touching my arm.

I left my bedroom in immaculate condition, but when I enter I discover my novels scattered about on rumpled bedsheets. An oversized marker with a pea green tip rests on my pillow. I notice on the cover of one of my books, a woman peers through a fractured window, her forehead scarred with barbed green symbols. On another cover, a man in a straw hat escapes a dark pit. A cloud of tumultuous spirals swarms about his face.

"Hello?" I say, glancing around the room again. But Mrs. Evers is nowhere to be seen.

While I'm packing, I remember the day Stephen finally left. I can still see him, cramming balled-up T-shirts into an already-stuffed suitcase. I asked him what the hell he thought he was doing, and he said he was going home for a while.

"Where's home?" I asked.

"Nevada," he said—where he grew up.

"You're really doing this? After everything?"

He glanced at me with the expressionless eyes of a supermarket cashier. "Yes."

"This isn't going to be forever," he told me. He said—

The memory jostles loose, because from somewhere under my bed comes a quivering whine. The sound intensifies with each passing moment. I picture Princess shivering on the floor, her brown lips frothing with yellow saliva. Her little legs kick and twitch.

Before I can investigate, Mrs. Evers squirms out from under the tall bed. She snorts, and her smiling eyes peek at me through a tangle of dark hair.

I take a long breath. "Robin said you wanted to speak with me?"

"Yeah," she says, ascending my bed with mud-crusted feet. As she jumps on the mattress, her ruffled sundress undulates and bobby pins rain down from her hair. "I gotta tell you a secret, Miss V. But we gotta go far away, or else he might hear us. He has ears like a wolf."

With that, she stretches out her arms like wings and springs off the bed. I gasp when she hits the floor at an awkward angle. She stumbles forward, ending up on her hands and knees. She giggles. As I help her up, I feel a mild urge to chastise her, the way I would one of my students. But of course I remain silent.

"Come on," she says, grabbing my hand. "My mom might wake up any time and then I'll get pushed out."

She tugs at my arm, but I plant myself on the floor. "Mrs. Evers, is this another one of your games? Like last night?"

"No!" she says. "We gotta hurry."

This time when she pulls at my arm, I let her tow me through the web of winding passageways. The scent of lavender follows us at every turn.

In one sunlit corridor, Mrs. Evers plays leapfrog over a parade of plastic zoo animals.

Ultimately, we end up in the garden of rock cress and buddleia and purple milkweed. I take a deep breath of the saccharine air. Mrs. Evers slips away from me and spins in circles on the grass.

As she twirls, she says, "Did you know rats can chew through metal and concrete? They can chew so much because their incisors never, ever stop growing. They have to keep chewing or their teeth will grow into their brains."

I sit on the wrought-iron bench, and my mind begins pulling me toward another age. I remember the parks, watching the boy while he rolled down the hills and covered his legs in sand and sang to the ducks. No. I force myself back into the present.

Mrs. Evers ends up resting on the base of the fountain. For some reason, the water is no longer flowing, and a monarch butterfly shivers on the tip of the warrior's marble spear.

The woman bites at her fingernail and says, "What are we doing here?"

I take a seat beside her. I place my hand on her back.

As if electrocuted by my touch, Mrs. Evers jumps and turns to me.

"This is where I died," she says. "I can't remember everything. It's so blurry."

A bright yellow swallowtail drifts in front of my eyes and then disappears.

"I fell right here," Mrs. Evers says, sprawling across the freshly cut grass. "I was alone for a long time, but then my dad came. My mom didn't come, because she was in the city, visiting Auntie Sharon." She rolls her head to the side, and I can see tears sparkling in the sunlight.

I kneel beside her.

"Dad said he tried to bring me back to life, but he couldn't. The men took me away in the ambulance, and I got burned up before Mom could see me. Dad should've let her hug me and say goodbye!"

"I'm sorry," I say.

She lies there, gazing at the sky, pulling out tufts of grass at her side. "Dad acts like he cares about us, but he's only pretending. One time, me and Mom and Dad were having a picnic, and I found a bird who couldn't fly. She was like this." For a few moments, she convulses in a frenzy on the grass. "When my dad saw her, he stomped her till she stopped moving, even though I was screaming. He said he could tell it was her time to go, and he didn't seem sad at all. He just cleaned off his shoe." She pinches the air above her face, maybe squishing the clouds above. "Another time, I had a nightmare about a wolf with a weird face. I went to tell Mom, but Dad said I should leave. I kept crying and I wouldn't go, and Dad looked really, really mad. His eyes were like a stranger. Dad carried me away and put me in a black room. I could hear Mom outside, trying to get me out, but Dad said I had to face the shadows or they would eat me up. I cried for a long time."

"That's awful," I say.

"Yeah." She looks at me now with wide, dusky eyes. She whispers, "The real truth is, my dad's not a real person. I saw him take off his face, and everything looked wrong. I don't know what he is, but he's getting stronger. Look." With this, Mrs. Evers uncovers a bruise on her chest in the shape of a crescent moon. "Mom's gotta run away or she might get eaten. You gotta warn her for me, Miss V. I can't talk to her because she sleeps whenever I go inside her. One time I tried writing her a message using her hand, but my letters are all weird. You gotta warn her about Dad."

A little voice tells me that I can't trust a word this woman says. She thinks she's a ghost. The bruise could be from anything.

But I already know I'm not going home. Not yet.

Mrs. Evers races off to dance around the jacaranda tree, and I sit watching, waiting for the other Mrs. Evers to wake up.

———

The wind yanks at my clothes as storm clouds envelop the sky like a linen shroud. Butterflies vanish. Mrs. Evers freezes in place, sniffing at the air. A small branch plummets to the ground and looks for a moment like a mangled claw.

Taking Mrs. Evers by the hand, I lead her inside, to the milk-warm sanctuary of my room. I close the door behind us and turn the lock. In a dark hollow of my mind, I imagine Mr. Evers lurking in the hallway, his face knotted and wrong.

"Can't we go in my room?" Mrs. Evers says. "I want to play in the cottage."

"Not now," I say.

The woman groans, and I hand over the plastic animals I scooped up on the way here. She grins. Almost immediately, the creatures begin shouting battle cries and go to war. A zebra with a British accent is the first to fall.

As the light in my room dims, I pick the bobby pins off my bed and place them in a neat pile on a mirrored vanity tray. My hand trembles with every action.

Thunder growls outside, and a small voice says, "It sounds close."

"We'll be fine," I say.

In the battle of the animals, a short-range missile blasts the rhino and elephant. The rhino clanks against the window and the elephant barely avoids hitting the eighty-four-inch, high-definition television. My mouth opens, and I almost tell Mrs. Evers not to throw things in the house. What do I think I'm doing?

After a few minutes, Mrs. Evers crawls over the carnage of the battlefield and climbs into my bed. She curls up in the shape of a crescent moon.

I drag a mahogany armchair to the side of the bed, and

the clamor of the storm intensifies.

"I hope the lightning hits the roof," Mrs. Evers says, wearing a small smile. Then she closes her eyes.

I sit, and watch her, and wait.

Soon, my focus drifts beyond the bed, to a headless child depicted in the stained-glass window. The girl or boy grapples with a demon-faced crow, shoving a hand into the creature's bulbous eye. When lightning flashes outside, the whole scene blazes, and I turn away.

Mrs. Evers sleeps without even the slightest movement. Absurdly, my heart rate surges until I'm able to perceive Mrs. Evers's chest rising and falling.

I take a deep breath. Another.

Grabbing one of my novels, I read the opening paragraph again and again. The author attempts to usher me into a churning metropolis where a woman in red maneuvers her body against the flow of foot traffic. I try to see what she sees, but the people and the buildings keep evaporating from my mind. Only certain words manage to anchor themselves inside me. Words like *emphysemic* and *abominable*.

I give up on the book when Mrs. Evers sits up suddenly, as if waking from a nightmare.

She glances around the room and her gaze pauses on my face. "Oh no," she says, in her natural voice. "Have I been wandering again? I'm so sorry for the intrusion, Ms.

Valdez. I'm afraid somnambulism runs in my family."

"It's all right," I say. "Before you go, I was wondering if we could speak for a moment?"

"Yes, of course," she says. She sits on the edge of the bed and stares at the clutter of animals on the floor. The wind murmurs at the window.

I say, "You . . . um . . . you spoke to me while you were sleepwalking."

She bites at a violet fingernail. "Oh?"

"Yeah." What am I supposed to say now? I study my hands, searching for answers. "You told me that Mr. Evers didn't let you see Isabella before she was cremated. Is that true?"

Mrs. Evers releases a soft snicker. "That is none of your business, Ms. Valdez. But if you must know, yes. Hubert knows how sensitive I am. He knew my heart would break to see my daughter that way. He only wanted to protect me."

"You told me he locked her in a dark room. He wouldn't let her out, even when she cried."

Mrs. Evers stares at me in silence, and lightning saturates the room with a dark blue radiance.

"You showed me the bruise on your chest," I say.

"That's nothing," Mrs. Evers says, in a cold, piqued tone. She stands and heads for the door.

"You seemed frightened," I say, following behind her.

"You can come with me, Mrs. Evers. We can leave this house right now."

Without turning, Mrs. Evers says, "I would never break up my family."

Then she lets out an awkward yelp and backs away from the door.

"Oh god, sweetie," she says, to the empty air. "You scared me."

Thunderclaps roll around us, like snarling dragons circling the house.

"I don't know what you're saying, sweetie. Calm down." The mother reaches out with trembling fingers and caresses nothing. Then she quickly pulls her hand away. "Oh god, sweetheart. Your face ... Please calm down! What do you want, sweetie?"

"She wants you to come with me," I say.

"She would never wish for me to leave our home."

"Listen to her."

"She can't speak!"

Mrs. Evers passes through the empty, spectral space in front of her, and I follow her into the hallway.

"Mrs. Evers, wait."

"Leave me alone," she says, her body dissolving into the shadows ahead.

As the storm lulls, I collect the vanquished zoo animals, and among them I discover a crinkled photograph of Isabella. A crown of lavender flowers rests on her dark curls. I place the photo on the mirrored vanity tray. Then I stand hugging my chest in the middle of the room. Should I speak with Mrs. Evers again? What else can I do for this woman? For now, I sit cross-legged on the disheveled bed and I attempt to read. The characters keep transforming into a girl with big brown eyes and an impish smile. Isabella anchors in my mind, as if to say, "Don't give up on us. Not yet."

I wake up on a soft bed with sunshine caressing half my face. For a moment or two, I expect to find Stephen sprawled out beside me like a gingerbread man. I expect his ratty socks and his feminine arms and his Boba Fett T-shirt. The memory brightens and then fades.

I'm in Stockton House. I am alone.

According to my phone, I only slept for a few minutes, but this feels wrong.

On my way to the servants' hall, I turn a sharp corner and nearly collide with Mr. Evers and his walking stick.

"Ms. Valdez," he says, grinning at my stomach and then my eyes. "I presumed you would be halfway to hearth and home by now."

I can feel a mishmash of emotions amassing in my

forehead, heating up my skin. Sweat slithers down my back.

"I changed my mind," I say, more quietly than I intend. "I'd like to help your wife."

The man's smile stretches farther across his clean-cut face. "This is wondrous news indeed. No doubt our little realm will benefit from your influence."

"I hope so. If you'll excuse me."

The man clears his throat and remains obstructing my path. "Before we part ways. I wonder if you have an inkling of my wife's whereabouts? The last I saw of her, she hurled insults at me and then retreated into the ether. I was just about to comb the grounds."

"I'm sorry," I say. "I don't know where she is."

He sighs. "Even in her altered state, Molly never used to spew such vitriol at me. I fear that she's losing the battle against whatever enervating shadows she has inside her." With a thumb, he massages the alabaster face that tops his walking stick. The carved head gapes at me with eyeless sockets and a wide open mouth. "I know she's not to blame for any of this, and yet . . . her transgressions always sting me to my core. How could they not? Before we lost Isabella, my Molly didn't have a dishonest or malicious bone in her body. My wife was never perfect, mind you. She spoiled Isabella, and she spoiled her husband, but she never . . ." His voice breaks, and he looks me in the eyes. "I'm droning on again, aren't I? I fear your countenance brings this out in me. Well, thank you for listening."

"I'll let you know if I find her," I say, trying to sound convincing.

The man smiles. He taps his walking stick on the floor. "Ah, before I forget. I would very much like to capture your likeness in one of my paintings. I will, of course, recompense you liberally for any hours you sacrifice posing in my chair. Whatever time you can spare would certainly satisfy my needs."

"No," I say, as an image of my portrait flashes in my mind. In the painting, my eyes coil together in a bloodshot spiral. My tongue squirms from a yawning nostril. "I'd rather not."

The light of his smile wanes. "Even an hour or two would suffice."

"No."

"Very well," Mr. Evers says. "If you change your mind, you know how to reach me."

The man grips his walking stick by the neck, and as he hurries past me, he grazes my arm with his own.

I take a deep breath. Another.

In the stairwell ahead, I ascend past the deformed faces etched into the walls. I observe savage, black scribbles on most of their foreheads. One of the women has her eyes blacked out. As I turn away from the image, I can feel the invisible hands on my shoulders, ready to twirl me around and push me down the stairs. I shut my eyes tight. The hands evaporate.

A stuffed beaver sits at the top of the stairs. She wears oversized pink sunglasses and holds a permanent marker under her paw.

I place the beaver on the dining table, next to the centerpiece of baby blue eyes.

Raul leans against the pool table, shifting the cue back and forth between his hands. He says, "I finally solved the mystery of the runaway capybara."

"Oh yeah?" I say.

"Yep. She was bit by a radioactive hummingbird."

"That is the only reasonable explanation."

Of course, I'm assuming that Mrs. Evers is the one responsible for the capybara's frequent escapes. Raul may not know about Mrs. Evers's psychological problems, so I keep the theory to myself.

"Robin said you need a ride into town?" Raul says, returning the pool cue to a red oak wall rack. "Are you ready to go?"

"I've decided to stay awhile."

"A wise choice," Raul says, and joins me at the table. "If you left now, you'd miss out on Robin's famous pulled pork."

"Heaven forbid."

The gardener plucks one of the wildflowers from the centerpiece and tucks it behind the beaver's ear. "Robin should be here in a few minutes," he says. "Care to play some pool while we wait?"

"Loser buys the winner a yacht?"

"Funny. I was thinking the same thing."

We play, and I already feel myself losing. One summer, I played pool every evening, but I can't quite invoke that girl with the frazzled jeans and the *Jem and the Holograms* T-shirt. I reach out, and the girl shrinks back into a thick fog.

After a long stretch of silence, I say, "Raul, I . . . if I asked you a question, could we keep it between us?"

Raul leans his pool cue against the table. "Yeah," he says. "Shoot."

"I was wondering if you've ever known Mr. Evers to act violently? Inappropriately?"

He rubs at the side of his neck. "Violently? No. I wouldn't say he's ever done anything especially inappropriate, but let's be honest—the guy is weird. I once told him that I'd rather not use any artificial plants in the gardens and he went off on a five-minute rant about how fake flowers are basically alive? Something like that. I don't understand half of what the guy says."

Within minutes, Robin arrives with her slow-cooker

pulled pork with apple slaw.

Robin says, "I didn't know if you'd still be with us, miss, but I prepared a plate for you just in case, thank heavens. I used mayonnaise for the slaw, instead of sour cream, so you can rest easy, miss."

"Thank you, Robin." I pick at a dried ketchup stain on the stuffed beaver's foot. "I've decided to stay and help the family. I'm going to need Mrs. Evers's cell number, so I can reach her more easily throughout the day."

The housekeeper studies my face for a few seconds and then nods. "Of course, miss. I can write that down for you, only you should know the Everses don't like to be disturbed after seven in the evening."

"I'll keep that in mind."

After lunch, I return to my room and discover the zoo animals once again strewn about the floor. Isabella's photograph lies on my pillow, with her eyes cut out. Chocolate fingerprints stain the bedsheets.

"Isabella?" I say.

I peek under the bed and search the adjoining bathroom. Nothing.

When I call the number Robin supplied me, the phone rings but no one answers. After the beep, I say, "This is Danna. Call me back."

I switch over to Isaac's texts, and for who knows how long, I scroll back in time. He's sent me a goat wearing a top hat and monocle. He's sent me a whole family with mullets. He's sent me a capybara in a tutu? No, that's a hamster.

With a mercurial thumb, I scroll back to the present.

I text, I DON'T KNOW IF I CAN HELP THIS TIME.

A little voice tells me to sit in bed for a while, and if I fall asleep, I fall asleep.

Instead, I sit in the uncomfortable armchair. For a few hours, I read, and I wait. An empty Toyota Corolla careens down the busy city street and hits the main character as she fantasizes about seducing her boss. Her body crumples. In her weakened state, a memory awakens inside her of a creature that lived under the floorboards of her grandmother's house. After a long recovery in the hospital, the main character visits her grandmother and discovers that the sallow creature still lives there. The creature's form remains nebulous, but I picture him with elongated limbs and a lipless mouth.

I rub my eyes.

After pocketing the book, I exit the room and wander the tortuous corridors of the house. I glance into open doorways. Sometimes I say, "Mrs. Evers?" And sometimes, "Isabella?" Every so often, I come across a plastic rat or a broken crayon. Sometimes I stop and shut my eyes tight. I listen for voices, but I can't hear anyone.

In time, I make my way outside and sit at the edge of

the fountain. An amber butterfly thrashes for survival in the placid water. I relocate her to the freshly cut grass, where her wings rise and fall and rise and fall. I open my book.

In the novel, the creature promises to grant Evangeline a wish if only she'll provide him with her pinky toe. He repeats this promise every day for months. Finally, she gives in, and she uses a hedge clipper to sever her flesh. She drops the sacrifice through a hole in the floor, and her wish is never granted. The creature squats in the dark, chewing, trembling with pleasure.

I look down to find the butterfly immobile on the grass, dead or gathering her strength.

"Isabella?" I say, to the vacant garden.

Wind caresses my bare skin as I follow a cobblestone path around the house. Birds burble, cloaked in the leaves above. I pass pillars topped with severed heads made of yellowing stone. Obsidian worms burst through the eyes of the statues, and the insects raise themselves toward the sky, like flowers reaching for sunlight.

Eventually, I end up in the hedge, shivering beside one of the Atrocities. The boy screams silently on his hands and knees. A round white stone rests on the top of his head, in a crater of fragmented bone. For a moment, he whispers to me, but it's only the wind in the leaves.

I call the number again.

This time, Mr. Evers answers. He says, "My wife is currently indisposed. Would you like to leave a message?"

"No. Thank you."

I hang up.

A little voice tells me I could keep walking. I could find my way out of this maze and I could escape this place.

Stockton House welcomes me back with an embrace of toasty air. For a few minutes, I stand in the foyer, breathing into my cupped hands. Then I continue rambling through the corridors and stairways and chambers. Soon, sunlight disentangles itself from the house. The brass fixtures above the hall paintings flicker to life, but for the most part the house darkens without interference.

I move in a sort of foggy trance until a distant clamor pulls me back to my present reality. I follow the sound into a drab, windowless hallway.

"Hello?" I say.

The banging stops, and Mrs. Evers says, "Miss V? You gotta get me out of here!"

I try the door at the end of the hall, but of course it's locked.

"They're gonna get me!" Mrs. Evers says. "They're coming out of the paintings. I can hear them breathing."

"That's only the wind," I say, with my hand against the door. "No one's going to hurt you."

"I keep telling Mom to wake up, but she won't. Why

won't she listen to me?"

"I don't know. Keep trying. Keep talking to her."

Mrs. Evers doesn't say anything for a while. Then, "Don't tell my dad, but I stole the extra keys. I gave them to Princess. I think she's in the schoolroom or the cottage or somewhere."

"Okay."

"Princess can protect you from him. She's not afraid of anybody."

I try to force the door open one more time. "I'll be back. Don't worry."

"Hurry. They're gonna come out."

As I turn away from the door, I can't help but picture the creature from my novel in the room, crouching low to the floor, gnawing on another toe. I push the thought away.

"Mom!" Mrs. Evers says, behind me. "Mom!"

I search Isabella's room after the schoolroom, and my eyes settle on the stuffed capybara sitting in a flower box, watching over the cottage like a guardian angel. Could this be the Princess Mrs. Evers was referring to? Underneath the animal I find a set of oversized brass keys.

When I return to the bleak hallway, I find the door to Mrs. Evers's prison wide open. I step into a dark room devoid of windows and furniture. Angels with patchwork faces glare down at me from the cement walls, and only a mouse-print blanket enlivens the floor. Mrs. Evers is nowhere to be seen.

I wait, and listen, and no one comes. Nothing happens.

I leave the brass keys under the blanket, just in case she's locked in here again while I'm away.

A few more minutes pass, and then I return to my room to organize my thoughts. A silver serving tray sits on my bedside table along with a handwritten note. *Dear Miss Danna,* Robin writes, *I don't know if I mentioned this, but I'm watching a movie in town tonight with my friend Michi. She's a sweet sort of person, only her taste in cinema puts my nose out of joint, as they say. I'll ask you, Miss Danna, what sort of person designates* Waterworld *as her favorite movie of all time? Not to be crude, but the man drinks his own urine. I suppose I prefer heroes with a little more decorum.* Robin goes on to describe the saffron pilaf and all the other dishes she prepared for me.

The pilaf tastes pleasant, though somewhat metallic.

I look at my phone. Isaac has texted back, OF COURSE YOU CAN HELP THEM, CUZ. YOU ALWAYS HELP THEM.

Even if I find a way to speak with Mrs. Evers again, what do I say? Should I call someone for help? Whom?

Before I can figure out my next step, I feel myself sinking. This isn't my medications tugging me gently into sleep. This is a new sensation. This is an invisible claw squeezing me tight, pulling me through my bed into the depths of the earth.

I try to open my eyes, but the darkness surrounds me, and fills me, and I am lost.

Minutes or hours or days later, a golden fulgor permeates my awareness. When I open my eyes, I observe Mr. Evers sitting at the edge of my bed, polishing his glasses with a bloodred handkerchief.

I attempt to sit up.

The man regards me with a melancholic smile. "I fear any attempts to reanimate your body will prove fruitless. Your flesh has already succumbed to the stresses of judgment, and your consciousness will follow before long."

"What have you done to me?" I want to say, but what escapes me is a trembling whine.

The man squeezes my ankle. "Hush now, Ms. Valdez. Even if you could manage a coherent plea for mercy, your words would fall on deaf ears. I have glimpsed the darkness in your soul, and your fate is now inescapable."

I scream for help, and the man forces a rectangle of duct tape over my mouth.

"You may find this difficult to believe, but I did everything in my power to prevent this moment. In a sense,

I consider our present situation as much a testament to my own shortcomings as yours." He sighs and pinches the bridge of his nose. "I vetted you and tested you to the best of my ability. I queried your references extensively. I welcomed you into my home because I came to the conclusion that your soul was unstained, and therefore impenetrable to damnation."

He stares at me now without expression.

"During the last inquisition in the dark room, Molly named you as a champion of sorts, sent here from on high to rescue her from captivity. She wasn't in her right mind, of course. Nevertheless, her confidence in you and your supposed crusade left me heavy with apprehension. To alleviate my fears, I decided to review the security footage from your room. And it was then, Ms. Valdez, that I discovered the truth about you." He grabs my leg again, tighter than before. "You enter my realm, and you conspire with my daughter's spirit to corrupt my wife? We have been nothing but hospitable and generous, and in return you wish to steal away my Molly and fracture my family?"

He releases me, and he gazes at the arm that rests limp and lifeless at my side. "Like most modern women, your arrogance blinds you to everything but the most superficial of realities. You see a wound on a woman's chest, and you perceive nothing of the love encapsulated in the mutilated flesh. You understand nothing of this house and our ways. You are a simpleminded creature whose sole function is to wreak havoc on holy bonds and sacred spaces. I would like to let you go, Ms. Valdez, but I'm duty-bound to facilitate in your fall." He clears his throat. "I do drone on, don't I? Well. I suppose now is as good a time as any to begin."

The man recedes for a moment, and returns with a medical syringe.

I can feel a hot tear sliding down my face. I try to turn away.

After he injects the crimson liquid into my arm, the room convulses, and a hairless, faceless woman lumbers through the open door. Her spindly arms slide beneath my neck and knees. Suddenly, a mouth splits her face in two like a wound. She grins. Mucusy insects wriggle their way through her tattered lips.

When she lifts me into her arms, I scream. I try to scream. She carries me through narrow corridors, and the walls blur past me, as if she's cantering down a moving sidewalk. Lights flicker. I'm little more than a statue at this point, but somehow I manage to turn my head toward the woman's face. For a moment, she closely resembles Mr. Evers, with the small glasses and the taciturn eyes. Tufts of mahogany hair sprout from her polished scalp and then recede. Spirals swirl on her forehead.

Once again, I face the onrushing hallway, and clusters of eyeballs open wide, growing inside the off-white walls. Amidst the eyes, mouths bare their black, craggy teeth.

I can see Robin crouching at the end of the hall, dropping pale potatoes into a steaming pot. Amber butterflies twitch underneath tight strands of Robin's hair, attempting to escape. Suddenly, I think of the saffron pilaf and the strange metallic taste. I think of the invisible claw that dragged me deep into the earth.

"You drugged me," I say, though with the duct tape over my mouth I can only speak with my thoughts. "You put something in my food."

"Yes, miss," Robin says.

"Yes, miss," the mouths in the wall echo. Obsidian worms slither through their ragged lips.

The housekeeper tosses a pair of tangled carrots into the pot, and I reach out and flick her. She flies backward, as if being pulled by a rope attached to a speeding vehicle. She crashes through a narrow window, effecting an explosion of stained-glass shards and butterfly wings.

What have I done? How could I even entertain the thought that she would betray me?

"Call an ambulance," I say. I try to say.

"Call an ambulance," the mouths repeat.

"Hush now, Ms. Valdez," the woman from the trumeau says. "There is nothing left for you to say."

Wirelike worms reach out from the walls and wind around my ankles and toes. I can feel them snaking up my thighs. Thankfully, the creatures withdraw as the faceless woman hauls me into a familiar hospital room with blanched walls. Shards of volcanic glass smolder on the tiled floor. I search the room for a bed, but I can't see one.

"Where is he?" I try to say.

"Where is he?" the mouths repeat, from afar.

I manage to turn my head slightly, and my eyes rest on a wound in the wall. Bluish-white veins pulse in the corroded drywall. Pus seeps from the cracks and collects in a pool on the floor. A featherless duck lies in the suppuration, dead or gathering his strength. I should go to him. I should bury him if he's gone. But I'm still a marionette with slackened strings.

Before long, a chasm opens in the floor. No, the chasm is a mouth. The woman conveys me into the hole, past rows of bleeding gums and decaying molars. The black worms live here too, thrashing in blood, burrowing into the soft flesh of the walls. The worms stretch out toward my feet, but they're too slow.

We travel down the precipitous steps, into the innards of the monstrosity. Soon, a tunnel of whirling fire looms before us. The sight should fill me with dread, shouldn't it? All I'm experiencing is a disconcerting calmness of mind and body. What's wrong with me?

We move through the passage, and I see naked arms piled in the flames. The severed limbs thrash and bend and blister. I see blackened moths drifting to the floor like cinders. When a fiery hand reaches out and brushes against my face, I expect to burn. Instead, I shiver in the cool air, and goosebumps swarm on my skin.

Further into the tunnel, a small, withered body convulses on a white blanket. His mouth opens wide. His skin ruptures and peels. Even after all these years, I can't do anything for him.

No, this can't be happening. I lower my eyes and I'm still wearing the vermillion cardigan, chartreuse floral dress, thin black belt. I must be awake.

In another moment, the roiling inferno closes in and swallows me whole.

———————

When I regain consciousness, wisps of smoke slither across my field of vision. I can feel my body shivering, but I still can't move my arms or legs. Is this death? Is this all that remains of my existence? A little voice tells me this is where I belong. This is what I deserve.

Slowly, the hazy miasma disperses, and can I make out a girl with big brown eyes and dark curls. She's no longer the roly-poly imp from the photograph. She stares at me with weary eyes, her features sharp and shrunken.

"Isabella?" I say. I try to say. What comes out of me is the chthonic wail of a creature living under the floorboards.

"Don't worry," the girl says. "You'll feel back to normal soon."

Black smoke still skulks in my periphery, but the world feels almost real again.

Isabella sits cross-legged on the cement floor, entertaining herself with tiny stone animals. The dog in her right hand hops over a pyramid of radishes and carrots and parsnips. "Good job," the girl says as a feeble smile flashes across her face.

When I try to sit up, the invisible hand presses down on my stomach. I ache as if I've just completed a hundred sit-ups.

"Isabella?" I say. I try to say. "Isabella?" The words finally flow from my lips, though they sound gritty and barbed.

The girl turns to me, balancing a stone horse on her head.

"Are you Isabella?"

"Yeah," she says. She bows her head slightly, allowing the mustang to slip into her hands.

My limbs scream at me, but I manage to crawl over and put my arms around the girl. She feels warm. She feels real. I can feel warm tears burning at my eyes.

"I'm going to get you out of here," I say.

"Do you know a way out?" Isabella says. "Albert always tried to find one, but he couldn't."

"Albert?"

The girl takes me by the hand and leads me deeper into the dank chamber. With every step, I can feel waves of fire and acid rushing up my legs. Bare bulbs hang from the ceiling, and Mr. Evers's painted angels gaze down on us from the stone walls. One of the portraits we pass resembles Isabella, but with her teeth pushing through her eyelids, and her gummy mouth opening in her neck. In addition to the angels, painted flames cover the walls, replete with burning faces and smoking flesh.

A man lies motionless in a dark corner of the chamber. A pair of small blankets cover his body, and his head's more beard than face. A burnt-out light bulb dangles above his head, like a forgotten idea.

"He's not feeling good," Isabella says.

I sit beside the man, grimacing with the pain this causes. He's still breathing. He's still warm.

Isabella kneels beside him and whispers, "Albert. Albert. A new lady is here."

Albert keeps his eyes closed.

"Who is he?" I ask, checking his pulse. I don't know what I'm checking for.

"He took care of the plants before Raul," the girl says, pinching at the ends of her hair. "Dad brought him here a long time ago."

My eyes rest on Albert's face again, and his lips appear like two shriveled slugs. Beads of sweat speckle his gray skin.

An invisible flame sears my face and chest. I can feel sweat forming on my forehead. I can feel my lips drying out. How long will it be before I'm lying on the cement beside him?

"I'll be right back," I say.

With slow, unsteady steps, I circumnavigate the gloomy chamber. Here and there, I press my hands against the wall, searching for secret passages, or perhaps I'm simply testing the boundaries of this reality. If the stones bend or scream or change color, I'll know that I'm dreaming or hallucinating.

Isabella walks beside me and says, "Did you know beavers have see-through eyelids? It's so they can see underwater. And they have lips behind their front teeth, not in front like us."

I find a few more blankets, and a platter of colorless carrots, and a toilet and sink tucked away in a small alcove. I find a metal door etched with spiraling vines and human eyes.

"There's a little sliding thing at the bottom," Isabella

says. "Dad puts the food through there."

I shove the door, and the metal does not bend or scream. I lower my eyes, and I'm still wearing the vermillion cardigan, chartreuse floral dress, thin black belt. I'm awake. I'm definitely awake.

My heart squirms and twirls. My heart is a whirlpool of flesh swirling around a murky vortex.

I continue my loop around the chamber, and Isabella stays with me for a while, holding my hand in silence. In time, she returns to her collection of stone animals. I should go and comfort her. I should tell her that everything will be all right.

I end up on the toilet, waiting for tears, searching my cardigan pockets for anything useful. All I discover is a note written in gold letters, in elegant uncials. The parchment paper reads: *In death, all misdeeds are forgiven.* It reads: *Please don't bang on the door. Please don't plug up the toilet.*

I crumple up the paper.

The tears I'm feeling never come, so I make my way back to Isabella.

I take a deep breath. Another.

"My name's Danna," I say. "I was wondering if you could tell me some more about beavers."

Isabella tells me everything she knows about beavers and lemmings and porcupines. And I tell her a story about a capybara who achieves her dream of becoming a prima ballerina of the Bolshoi Ballet.

After the story, we return to Albert's side. Isabella gives him a little water from a wooden bowl.

Rubbing my aching legs, I say, "You said your father brings you food through the door. Have you told him that Albert's sick?"

"Yeah," the girl says.

"What does he say?"

She places the bowl next to Arnold's head. "It doesn't matter to him. Dad says we're already dead."

"Has your father ever—"

I never finish the sentence, because a cacophonous clank invades the room. And the metal door begins to open. I picture Mr. Evers stepping through, dressed in blue jeans and a beige smock, speckled with blood.

I stand. Isabella stands.

Instead of Mr. Evers, his wife appears in the doorway and says, "Bell!"

When she rushes to her daughter, the door starts to close, so I hurry forward and shove it with both hands. The metal still won't scream or change color, but I don't care anymore. I hold the door wide open.

"We need to leave," I say.

Molly holds her daughter close. "Are you real? Are you real?"

"Yeah," the girl says.

"We need to go now," I say. "Mrs. Evers—Molly! Isabella."

Isabella takes her mother by the hand and leads her out of the chamber. I let the door close behind us, revealing a three-pronged spindle wheel on the opposite side. We travel a cement tunnel painted with towering flames and blistered flesh.

"What about Albert?" Isabella says.

"We'll send help for him soon," I say.

We reach the end of the flames and begin climbing a lofty flight of stairs.

"I'm so, so sorry," Mrs. Evers says. "We should have left years ago, but I didn't know he was a monster until tonight. He locked me in the dark room, and I finally heard you, Bell. I heard you inside me. But was that you?"

"Mom?" Isabella says, her voice shaky.

"You said he could take off his face," Molly says. "You said he might devour me if I didn't run away. So I . . . I escaped and I followed him. I wanted to see the truth for myself. And I saw him carry you down here, Ms. Valdez."

"Is he still nearby?" I ask.

"No, no," the woman says, waving the thought away. "I waited until he went back to bed, and then I made my way through the tunnel. But how is it that you're alive, Bell? You told me you were dead. You showed me where you collapsed."

"I'm fine, Mom."

At the top of the stairs, we pass through an opening in the floor into Mr. Evers's unlit studio. My heart climbs into my throat when I notice a woman sitting on the velvet armchair, in front of the muslin backdrop. She stares blankly in our direction, her hands raised high in the air, her fingers curled.

Isabella must notice what I'm looking at, because she whispers, "That's only his dummy."

The woman's face seems to contort, but that's only a trick of the moonlight. A trick of my mind.

"We should call the police," I say.

Mrs. Evers whispers, "He took my phone when he locked me away. I assume he took yours as well. We don't own a landline."

The floor creaks somewhere nearby, and our bodies freeze like the mannequin in the armchair. We wait. Mr. Evers doesn't appear.

We creep together through the hallways, passing angels and spirals and wide open eyes. And I finally see Stockton House for what it is. Mr. Evers uses the symbols above to rationalize his dungeon below, and it's all bullshit. There's nothing here but bullshit.

Once we pass through the black wood doors, I take a deep breath. Another.

We move forward. On either side of us, colossal faces sculpted in the hedges scream their silent screams. Moonlight alone lights our path.

We've almost reached the maze when Isabella says, "Mom, what are you doing?"

Mrs. Evers is facing the house again, her hands at her cheeks. "Oh god. We have to go back."

"What's wrong?" I say.

"Don't you see?" She points to the battered facade where headless figures claw at the darkness. "Your soul is still in there with him, Bell. Right there in the window. Don't you see?"

"Isabella's right here," I say. "She's safe. We need to keep moving."

"Come on, Mom," Isabella says.

Mrs. Evers squeezes the fingers of her left hand with her right hand.

I catch a glimpse of movement in the corner of my eye, and I turn in time to see the front door of Stockton House swing open. Mr. Evers appears, dressed in a shimmering silk robe. He's holding a medical syringe in one hand and a kitchen knife in the other.

"Wait right there," he says. "Do not move."

"Hide," I say to Isabella, but she doesn't move.

I look around for something, anything. A rock? A trowel? Raul's Lesche knife? I see nothing.

Mr. Evers approaches us swiftly, and I take Isabella by the hand, ready to run.

"Stay away from us, Hubert," Mrs. Evers says. "Let us go."

"You don't understand," the man says, stopping a few yards from us. Tears well up in his eyes. "You know my heart, Molly. You know I find no greater joy than giving you everything you desire. However, I can't give you our daughter, because she is beyond our reach. The creatures who stand beside you are not the people you knew. As soon as they crossed the threshold into the unearthly realm, their physical forms transmogrified into little more than solidified ectoplasm. They're abominations, Molly. And their being here in the realm of men is an affront to every rule that binds our reality together." He gestures wildly with the knife, cutting the skin beside his right eye. "For now, I'm utilizing every ounce of my willpower to minimize the damage they're causing. But if they escape my sphere of influence, there's no telling what will become of our world. The very fabric of time and space might unravel." He points the knife in my direction. "You must let me have them, Molly. They are nothing to you. They are walking corpses, held together by memories and dreams."

"Put down the knife, Hubert," Mrs. Evers says. "I need to speak with you privately for a moment."

She walks forward, and Mr. Evers keeps his weapons at his side.

As soon as she's close enough, Molly kicks the man hard between the legs. Then, when he crumples, she kicks him hard in the face.

"Ahh," he says. "Ahh. Ahh."

Without thinking, I race forward and grab the fallen knife. I take a step closer to the man. I raise the blade slightly.

And I can feel Isabella watching me. I can feel Bruno.

"Ahh," the monster says, writhing on the grass. "Ahh."

I turn away from the man, and we hurry into the maze.

"Follow me," Isabella says.

Hand in hand in hand, we pass the boy with the crater in his skull, and the man with the bleeding sores, and the woman with the collapsing face. Before long, we hear a car. More specifically, we hear a small utility vehicle with cushioned seats and integrated cup holders.

"You're here, miss," Robin says to the girl, as she hops out of the vehicle. She's wearing a pink wool coat and a feathered hat.

"Yeah," Isabella says.

Robin and I sit cross-legged in the bed of the UTV so that the mother and daughter can sit up front with Raul. A mellow breeze cools my face. The air smells like lavender. We work our way through the labyrinth, leaving the Atrocities behind us.

In time, I can feel the darkness of sleep closing in. Robin chatters beside me about 3-D projectors. Mrs. Evers sings a lullaby about dancing fish. Isabella giggles.

As I close my eyes, the voices surround me, and fill me, and I feel alive.

Acknowledgments

Many thanks to Lee Harris, Sam Araya, Christine Foltzer, and everyone on the Tor.com Publishing team who helped make this book possible. Thank you to my family, for being lovely, supportive people who are quite unlike all the chthonic family figures in my stories. Thanks to Lisa for expanding and galvanizing my love of gothic fiction. And I am forever grateful to my local libraries, for supplying copious worlds to explore, and for providing the perfect space to sit and think and create weird little worlds of my own.

About the Author

Photograph by Jacob Shipp

JEREMY C. SHIPP is the Bram Stoker Award–nominated author of *Cursed, Vacation,* and *Sheep and Wolves.* His shorter tales have appeared or are forthcoming in more than seventy publications, including *Cemetery Dance, ChiZine,* and *Shroud Quarterly.* Jeremy lives in Southern California in a moderately haunted Victorian farmhouse. His Twitter handle is @JeremyCShipp.

TOR·COM

Science fiction. Fantasy. The universe.

And related subjects.

More than just a publisher's website, *Tor.com* is a venue for **original fiction, comics,** and **discussion** of the entire field of SF and fantasy, in all media and from all sources. Visit our site today—and join the conversation yourself.